W9-AGH-242

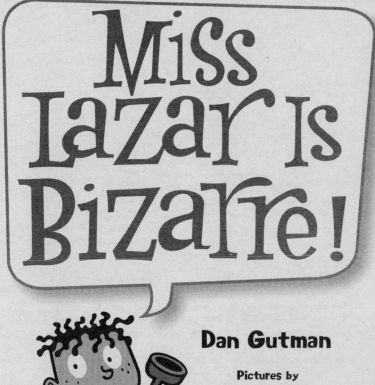

Miss Lazar Is Bizarre!

Dan Gutman

Pictures by
Jim Paillot

HarperTrophy®
An Imprint of HarperCollinsPublishers

Miss Lazar Is Bizarre!

Text copyright © 2005 by Dan Gutman

Illustrations copyright © 2005 by Jim Paillot

Library of Congress Cataloging-in-Publication Data

Gutman, Dan.

   Miss Lazar is bizarre! / Dan Gutman ; pictures by Jim Paillot.—1st ed.

     p.   cm. — (My weird school ; #9)

   Summary: A.J. and his friends find out what amazing things Miss Lazar, the Super Custodian at their school, can do.

   ISBN-10: 0-06-082225-2 (pbk.) — ISBN-10: 0-06-082226-0 (lib. bdg.)

   ISBN-13: 978- 0-06-082225-5 (pbk.) — ISBN-13: 978- 0-06-082226-2 (lib. bdg.)

   [1. Janitors—Fiction. Schools—Fiction.] I. Paillot, Jim, ill. II. Title. III. Series: Gutman, Dan. My weird school ; #9.

PZ7.G9846Mkm 2005   2005014974

[Fic]—dc22

❖

First Harper Trophy edition, 2005

Visit us on the World Wide Web!

www.harperchildrens.com

16 17 OPM 30 29 28

To Emma

Contents

A Bathroom Emergency

My name is A.J. and I hate school.

Listen, I'm about to tell you something I never told anyone else. I never even told my best friends, Michael and Ryan.

But you can't tell *anyone*. It's a secret. Promise? Cross your heart and hope to die? Are you ready? Okay, here's the secret.

I can't tell you.

Oh, all right, I'll tell you.

Sometimes, when I'm at school, I ask my teacher, Miss Daisy, if I can go to the bathroom even though I don't really have to go to the bathroom. That's the secret.

Okay, okay, so it isn't such a great secret.

But sometimes I just get that antsy feeling, and I want to get out of class for a few minutes. So I ask to go to the boys' room.

I was feeling that antsy feeling one day in class. Miss Daisy was talking about weather, and she was showing us pictures of volcanoes and tornadoes. It was pretty cool, but I just wanted to stretch my legs for a few minutes. So I raised my hand and asked Miss Daisy if I could go to the boys' room. She said okay.

Nobody else was in the boys' room. I didn't have much to do in there. There's not a whole lot to do in a bathroom, except for go to the bathroom, which I didn't have to do. I looked in the mirror for a minute and made funny faces. I washed my hands. I shot paper towels at the garbage can. Then I figured I'd better get back to class.

I thought I should flush the toilet because then it would sound like I really went to the bathroom. So I flushed it.

You know how the water is supposed to swirl around and around the toilet bowl like a little tornado and then go down the hole in the bottom? Well, this water didn't swirl at all. It didn't go down the hole, either. It just started rising.

It got higher.

And higher.

It went all the way up to the very edge of the bowl. I started to panic. And then it went *over* the edge and started spilling onto the floor! Water was pouring out of the toilet bowl! It looked just like those erupting volcanoes Miss Daisy was telling us about. I thought I was gonna die.

I didn't know
what to say. I
didn't know what to do. I had
to think fast. So I ran out of the
boys' room and started yelling.

"Help! There's a volcano in the boys'
room! Run for your life! It's erupting! The
toilet is going to explode!"

Everybody came running out
of our class, even Miss
Daisy. Our principal, Mr.

Klutz, was down the hall. He came running over too.

"What's going on?" asked Mr. Klutz, who has no hair on his head at all. I mean *none*. His head is like a big lightbulb.

"I flushed . . . and the water . . . it got higher . . . and it's going to blow!" I panted. I was all out of breath.

Mr. Klutz pulled out his walkie-talkie and started talking into it. "Miss Lazar!" he said. "Come quickly to the boys' bathroom! It's an emergency!"

Miss Lazar to the Rescue

Now the water was sliding under the boys' room door and into the hallway! The whole school was going to be flooded!

For a second or two, I thought, *This is great!* If the school flooded, we would get to go home. Maybe the erupting toilet volcano wasn't such a bad thing after all.

"Did you put something down the toilet, A.J.?" Mr. Klutz asked me.

"No!" I said. "I just flushed it, and—"

I never got the chance to finish my sentence, because at that very moment there was an ear-piercing shriek of a whistle, and it sounded like a lawn mower was coming down the hallway.

It was Miss Lazar, our school custodian! She was riding her motorized scooter. Miss Lazar was wearing her big blue overalls with the letters "SC" on the front. She carried one of those toilet plunger thingies with a suction cup on the end. My parents have one at home just like it.

Miss Lazar and the scooter screeched to a stop right in front of us.

"Have no fear, students! It is I, Super Custodian!" said Miss Lazar as she hopped off the scooter. "What happened?"

"A.J. had a bathroom emergency," said Andrea Young, this really annoying girl in my class with curly brown hair who I hate.

"I did not!" I said.

"You got here just in time, Miss Lazar!" said Mr. Klutz. "The toilet must have backed up."

Mr. Klutz totally didn't know what he was talking about. The toilet didn't back up. It didn't move an inch.

"This looks like a job for Super Custodian!" said Miss Lazar.

"What a mess," Andrea said. "A.J. made a big mess."

"The messier the better," said Miss Lazar. "I love messes!"

"You do?" I asked. "Why?"

"If kids didn't make any messes, I wouldn't have a job," said Miss Lazar. "So make all the messes you want. In fact, I wish you kids would throw more garbage on the floor. I don't have enough to clean up."

So nah-nah-nah boo-boo on Andrea.

"Stand aside, students," said Miss Lazar. "Super Custodian is here to save the day! Anytime fingerpaint is spilled, or somebody loses a retainer in the garbage can, or a child throws up, I am at your service to—"

"Can you just clean up the mess, please?" asked Mr. Klutz.

"You can count on me!" Miss Lazar said. She put on these gigantic yellow plastic gloves and pushed open the boys' room door. It looked like a lake in there.

Miss Daisy told us we should go back to our classroom. But before we could make a move, we heard Miss Lazar's voice.

"Aha!" she shouted. "Here's the problem!"

Miss Lazar came back out of the bathroom with something in her hand.

"Crayons!" she said. "Somebody stuffed a bunch of crayons down the toilet."

Mr. Klutz and Miss Daisy looked at me like I was the one who stuffed the crayons down the toilet. I didn't. I really didn't. Why would I do a dumb thing like that?

From the hallway we could see the water was starting to go down the drain in the bathroom floor. The toilet wasn't overflowing any-more.

"Wow, you did it, Miss Lazar!" said Andrea. What a brownnoser!

"Miss Lazar saved the day!" said Andrea's crybaby friend, Emily. Everybody started cheering and clapping their hands. Miss Lazar took a bow.

Principal Klutz is like the king of the school, but Miss Lazar is like a real living superhero. Anytime something goes wrong anywhere in the school, she is the person to call. Miss Lazar can clean up any mess and fix anything that breaks. She's the only one in the whole school who can turn the lights on and off when we have an assembly, because she has a special key. She can solve just about any problem in the world.

"It was nothing, really," said Miss Lazar, taking off her yellow gloves. "Anybody could have–"

She never got the chance to finish her sentence, because at that very moment her walkie-talkie beeped.

"Miss Lazar!" said the voice in the walkie-talkie. "We have an emergency in Mr. Docker's science room!"

"Until we meet again!" said Miss Lazar as she hopped back on her scooter. "Duty calls!"

And then she roared down the hallway.

Me and Michael and Ryan started giggling because Miss Lazar said "duty," and the word "duty" sounds exactly the same as the word "doody." It's okay to say "duty," but you're not supposed to say "doody." So every time anybody says "duty," I can't help but think of "doody," and I have to start giggling.

"Duty" sounds way too much like "doody," if you ask me. Those two things should definitely have two different words. Don't you think?

3

The Greatest Idea in the History of the World

After all the excitement was over, we went back to class and learned more about weather. Miss Daisy said she was proud of the way I made a connection between volcanoes and tornadoes and toilet bowls. That made me feel good. But then an announcement came over the loudspeaker that made me feel bad.

"Students, this is a reminder that you should never put crayons or any other inappropriate objects into the toilet bowls. Thank you!"

Everybody looked at me. I didn't put *anything* down the toilet bowl. I didn't even have to go to the bathroom in the first place.

Luckily it was time for recess. Me and Michael and Ryan climbed the monkey bars. Annoying Andrea and Emily were playing catch nearby with a tennis ball.

"I bet I know why you put crayons down the toilet, A.J.," Andrea said. "You were trying to start a flood so school

would be closed and you could go home."

What is her problem? Why can't a toilet bowl fall on her head?

That was a total lie she made up. I didn't even *think* of flooding the school so we could go home until the bathroom

was already flooded. I just ignored Andrea.

"Tell us the truth," Ryan whispered. "Were you the one who put crayons down the toilet?"

"You can admit it to us, A.J.," said Michael. "We won't tell anybody."

"Guys," I said, "I didn't put *anything* down the toilet. I didn't even have to *go* to the bathroom. I just wanted to get out of class for a few minutes."

Andrea and Emily were still throwing their tennis ball back and forth.

"You hate school," Andrea said. "That's why you did it, A.J."

"You're gonna get in trouble," Emily said.

"I didn't do it!" I yelled.

"Did too!"

We went back and forth like that for a while, until the tennis ball that they were playing catch with got loose. It rolled over near the monkey bars. I jumped down and grabbed it.

"Toss me the ball, A.J.," Andrea said, holding her hands out.

Well, nah-nah-nah boo-boo on her. Because that's when I got the greatest idea in the history of the world. I didn't toss the tennis ball back to Andrea. I took that ball and chucked it up on the roof of the school!

"Oops," I said to Andrea. "Sorry. I missed you. Bad throw."

"Way to go, A.J.!" said Ryan.

"Wow, I didn't know you could throw that far," said Michael.

Emily started crying, the big crybaby. "That's *my* tennis ball!" she said. "I got it for my birthday. It's a special ball that glows in the dark."

"Now you're *really* going to be in trouble," Andrea said. "First you stuffed crayons in the toilet, and now you threw Emily's ball up on the roof. I'm going to tell on you. My mother is vice president of the PTA, you know. She could have you suspended."

"She means it, A.J.," said Ryan.

"If you get suspended, you still have to do all your classwork," Michael said.

He must have been reading my mind, because as soon as Andrea said I would be suspended, I started thinking it would be cool to sit home and play video games all day.

"Okay, okay," I said to Emily. "I'll get your stupid glow-in-the-dark tennis ball back."

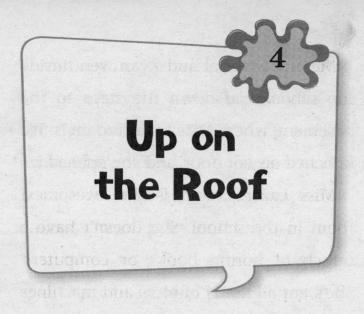

Up on
the Roof

How was I going to get Emily's ball back? There were no ladders or stairs leading up to the roof of the school. I didn't know how to get up there. There was only one thing to do. I had to go find Miss Lazar. She would be able to figure out how to get up there.

Me and Michael and Ryan went inside the school and down the steps to the basement, where Miss Lazar's room is. We knocked on her door, and she opened it.

Miss Lazar's room is the awesomest room in the school. She doesn't have a bunch of boring books or computers. She's got all kinds of tools and machines and junk all over the place. It is cool.

In the corner I noticed a door with a sign on it that said SECRET ROOM. Wow! A secret room! My friend Billy who lives around the corner told me that every school has a secret room down in the basement. Billy says that's where they keep the bad kids.

"What's in the secret room?" Ryan asked Miss Lazar.

"That's where I keep the bad kids," said Miss Lazar.

Billy was right!

But then Miss Lazar laughed and said she was just joking. She told us she had something very special in the secret room, but she couldn't tell us what it was because, if she did, it wouldn't be secret.

We told Miss Lazar that some kid (not me) threw a tennis ball up on the roof of the school.

"This looks like a job for Super Custodian!" said Miss Lazar, grabbing her toilet bowl plunger. She stuck it into her belt like a sheriff in a western movie sticks his gun in a holster.

"Why do you need a toilet bowl plunger to get a tennis ball off the roof?" I asked.

"Oh, you never know when a plunger might come in handy," Miss Lazar said. She's weird.

Miss Lazar marched out to the play-ground, and we followed her. She looked up at the roof, and then she looked at the wall of the school. Then she did the most amazing thing in the history of the world. She started climbing the wall!

Everybody in the playground stopped what they were doing and ran over to watch. Miss Lazar dug her fingers and the toes of her shoes into the little cracks between the bricks, and she slowly made her way up the wall. It was amazing! You should have been there!

I guess word got around, because by the time Miss Lazar reached the second floor of the school, even Mr. Klutz had come out to watch.

"What's going on?" Mr. Klutz asked.

"Miss Lazar is climbing up to the roof to get Emily's tennis ball," Ryan told him.

"I used to do a little rock climbing

in my younger days," Mr. Klutz said.

Finally Miss Lazar was standing up on the roof of the school. Everybody was craning their neck to see her.

"There are all *kinds* of things up here!" Miss Lazar called down. Suddenly balls and notebooks and hats and other stuff were flying off the roof.

"There's my old Frisbee!" some kid yelled.

"I was *wondering* where that umbrella went," said somebody else.

Emily got her stupid ball back. Everybody clapped and cheered for Miss Lazar as she climbed back down the wall.

"Wow, Miss Lazar is like Spider-Man!" one of the third graders hollered.

"Okay, everyone," Mr. Klutz said, clapping his hands. "The show is over, and so is recess. Everyone back to class now."

"Boooooooo!"

"Hooray for Miss Lazar!" somebody yelled.

"Hip hip hooray!" we all shouted.

"Nothing to it," Miss Lazar said when she got to the bottom. "Time to mop the cafetorium. Duty calls."

Then we all giggled because Miss Lazar said "duty" again.

A Visit from Mr. Klutz

When we came back to class, I noticed that this kid named Robbie who sits in front of me was missing.

"Where's Robbie?" I asked Miss Daisy.

"His mother came to pick him up," she said. "Robbie wasn't feeling well."

That was weird. Robbie never told

anyone he was sick.

Miss Daisy asked us to clear off our desks and be on our best behavior, because Mr. Klutz was coming in to talk with us.

Soon Mr. Klutz came in with his bald head. It is *so* shiny! He must wax it or something. Mr. Klutz is weird.

"Hello, second graders," Mr. Klutz said. "I came in to tell you about a new program at Ella Mentry School. We're going to become a MEAN school."

"That doesn't sound very nice," said Andrea Young.

"MEAN stands for Make Excellence A Necessity," said Mr. Klutz. He wrote

MEAN on the chalkboard and told us that all the parents and teachers and students were going to work really hard so our school would be rated the smartest school in the whole state. Mr. Klutz went on and on about the MEAN program. I wasn't paying much attention. It was really boring.

Finally Mr. Klutz finished talking, and he asked if any of us had questions. I raised my hand, and he called on me.

"Does Miss Lazar have super powers?"

"Uh, no, A.J.," Mr. Klutz said. "She's just a regular custodian."

"Regular?" asked Ryan. "Then how did she climb the wall?"

"That was simple rock climbing," Mr. Klutz said. "It's not that difficult."

"Miss Lazar is cool," some kid said.

"That's not a question," said Mr. Klutz. "Does anyone have any *questions*?"

"Is the toilet in the boys' bathroom haunted?" I asked.

You see, my friend Billy around the corner once told me that sometimes a toilet will overflow because there's a ghost inside it pushing the water out.

"Of course the toilet is not haunted,"

said Mr. Klutz. "Don't be silly."

"That was cool when Miss Lazar fixed the toilet," Michael said.

"That's not a question, Michael," said Mr. Klutz.

"That was cool when Miss Lazar fixed the toilet, wasn't it?" Michael asked.

"Yeah," everybody agreed.

"Okay, that's enough about Miss Lazar," said Mr. Klutz. "Does anyone have any *other* questions?"

"Mr. Klutz, do you wish you were Super Custodian instead of being a plain old boring principal?" Ryan asked.

"I have to go now," said Mr. Klutz.

The Haunted Toilet Bowl

I don't know exactly how it happened. I guess some kid in my class told some kid in another class that the toilet in the boys' bathroom was haunted. That kid told some other kid, and that kid told some other kid. By two o'clock, everybody in school was talking about the ghost in the toilet bowl.

None of the boys wanted to go in the boys' room. I wouldn't want to go into a boys' room if there was a ghost in the toilet bowl. Would you?

Usually Miss Daisy lets us go to the boys' room after lunch. But none of us wanted to go in there. I figured I'd wait until I got home. All the boys in school were holding it in all day. We thought we were gonna explode!

"Boys, will you please go to the boys' room?" Miss Daisy said.

"No!" all of us boys replied. "There's a ghost in the toilet!"

"Then use the girls' room," she said.

"No way!" I said. "The girls' room has cooties."

None of the boys in the school wanted to go to the boys' room. It must have been another bathroom emergency, because Mr. Klutz called all the boys in the whole school into the gym to talk to us.

"I promise you, the boys' bathroom is *not* haunted," Mr. Klutz announced. "I have been in there. There is *no*

40

ghost in the toilet. It is perfectly safe to use the bathroom."

"I don't believe you," some fifth grader yelled.

"Me neither," said somebody else.

"I bet Miss Lazar would know if the bathroom is haunted," Ryan said. "She knows everything."

"Yeah!" Michael agreed.

Everybody started chanting, "Miss Lazar! Miss Lazar! Miss Lazar!" It was cool.

Mr. Klutz called Miss Lazar on his walkie-talkie, and we all cheered when she rode into the gym on her scooter. She had her toilet bowl plunger with her, as usual.

"This looks like a job for Super Custodian!" said Miss Lazar.

"Is the boys' room haunted, Miss Lazar?" asked Mr. Klutz.

"Of course not," said Miss Lazar.

"So you killed the ghost that was in the toilet bowl?" some first grader asked.

"There was no ghost in the toilet bowl," Miss Lazar said.

"Miss Lazar is just being modest," said Ryan.

"Hooray for Miss Lazar!" somebody yelled. "She killed the ghost!"

"SHE KILLED THE GHOST!" everybody started chanting. "SHE KILLED THE GHOST!"

"Now we can use the boys' room again!" I yelled.

"Hip hip hooray for Miss Lazar!" everybody shouted.

I thought Mr. Klutz would be happy, but he looked like he was all mad about something. One of the fourth graders raised his hand and Mr. Klutz called on him.

HiP HiP HooRay!

"May I please go to the boys' room?" the kid asked.

"Yes!" Mr. Klutz yelled. "Go! That's what I've been trying to tell you to do!"

Every boy in the school started running for the boys' room like they were giving out free candy in there. It was cool.

Miss Lazar's Secret Identity

The next day that kid Robbie who sits in front of me didn't come to school again. Miss Daisy told us he had chicken pox, which is a dumb disease that makes no sense because you can get it even if you never touch a chicken.

After we finished pledging the

allegiance, we made get-well cards for Robbie. Andrea made a picture of a smiling Robbie with butterflies and flowers around him. I made a picture of Robbie sword fighting with a chicken and chopping its head off.

While we were drawing our pictures,

we started talking about Miss Lazar.

"Do you think Miss Lazar is a real superhero?" Ryan asked.

"Well, she *did* kill the ghost in the toilet," Michael said. "So we know she has super powers."

"She's got a uniform with letters on it too," I said. "Superheroes always wear cool uniforms."

"They always have a secret place they go when they need to be alone," said Ryan. "Miss Lazar has a secret room down in the basement."

I didn't think Andrea and her little nosy girlfriends were listening to us, but of course they were.

"You boys are silly dumbheads," said Andrea. "Miss Lazar isn't a superhero."

"Yeah," agreed Emily. "She's just a custodian."

Andrea thinks she knows everything. But I bet I know a whole lot more about superheroes than she does, because I have lots of superhero comic books at home. And I was sure that Miss Lazar was a superhero.

"Maybe Miss Lazar isn't a custodian at all," I said. "Did you ever think of that? Superheroes always have a secret identity. Like Superman is really Clark Kent, and Batman is really Bruce Wayne, and Spider-Man is really Peter Parker.

Maybe being a custodian is just Miss Lazar's secret identity."

"Yeah," said Ryan. "And maybe Robbie doesn't really have chicken pox, either. Maybe he's locked in the secret room in Miss Lazar's office. Stuff like that happens all the time, you know."

"Maybe Robbie was the kid who put the crayons down the toilet," I said. "Maybe he got caught. Miss Lazar told us she keeps the bad kids in the secret room."

"Stop trying to scare Emily!" said Andrea.

"Remember last year when that kid Steven moved away?" Michael asked. "Maybe he didn't move away at all. Maybe he was bad. Maybe Steven and Robbie are locked in the secret room in Miss Lazar's office."

"We've got to do something!" said Emily, and she went running out of the class. Emily is weird.

Miss Daisy collected our cards and told us to clean off our desks because it was time for math. I hate math. We are learning multiplication, which makes no sense at all.

"Miss Daisy, I don't understand the three times table," this girl named Annette said.

"Me neither," said Miss Daisy, who doesn't know anything. "But don't tell Mr. Klutz. If he finds out I can't do math, I'll get fired."

Everybody was trying to teach Miss Daisy the three times table. We put three pencils on her desk and told her three times one is three. Then we put three more pencils on her desk and told her three times two is six. Then we put three more pencils on her desk and told her three times three is nine.

"I don't get it," said Miss Daisy. She must be the dumbest teacher in the history of the world. We had to show her all over again.

While we were doing math, I was thinking about something much more important—Miss Lazar. If she was really a superhero pretending to be a custodian, there was one sure way to find out.

We had to sneak into Miss Lazar's secret room down in the basement.

The Secret of the Secret Room

I wrote this note and slipped it to Michael:

Meet after school by the big turtle. We can sneak into Miss Lazar's secret room. Pass note to Ryan.

Michael read the note and gave me the thumbs-up sign. Then he passed the note over to Ryan. Ryan read the note and gave me the thumbs-up sign. Then he put the note in his mouth and started chewing it. Ryan will eat anything, even stuff that is not food. He's weird.

At the end of the day, me and Michael and Ryan met in the playground near the big turtle.

"I just saw Miss Lazar mopping the vomitorium," said Michael. "She'll be there at least a half an hour."

"Let's go!" I said.

We snuck back in the school through the side door, being quiet like mice. We tiptoed down the steps to the basement.

"Hey, why did you eat the note?" I whispered to Ryan.

"I had to destroy the evidence so it wouldn't fall into the wrong hands," said Ryan. "I saw somebody do that in a movie once."

"Good thinking," I said, even though I think Ryan just likes eating paper.

"Shhh!" Michael shushed.

We slid against the walls and crouched down low so nobody would see us. We were like real secret agents, except we didn't have guns or trench coats. It was cool.

The door to Miss Lazar's office was wide open. We went inside.

"Quick!" Ryan said. "Somebody could come in any minute."

I went to the door of the secret room. It

was closed. I put my hand on the knob. It turned. I pulled open the door.

It was a little room, not much bigger than a closet. It was dark in there. We couldn't see much. Something was hanging on the walls.

"Turn on the light," said Michael. I found a switch on the wall.

You'll never guess in a million hundred years what was hanging all over the walls in Miss Lazar's secret room.

I'm not going to tell you.

Okay, okay, I'll tell you.

Toilet bowl plungers!

There must have been about twenty of them! There were big plungers and little plungers. Fat plungers and skinny

plungers. Plungers in every color. Some of them had little cards next to them explaining what company made the plunger or what year it was made.

It was like a museum of toilet bowl plungers!

"Wow!" I said. "Miss Lazar really likes toilet bowl plungers!"

My mom collects glass paperweights, and my uncle Eric collects old radios, but I never heard of anyone who collected toilet bowl plungers. That's a weird thing to collect.

We closed the door to the secret room and got out of there fast.

Miss Lazar is bizarre!

9

Sad, Depressed Mr. Klutz

We were in the vomitorium eating lunch the next day. I gave Michael my tuna sandwich, and Ryan gave me his cookies. I told Ryan that he might want to eat a few napkins for dessert, because he likes eating paper so much. He said I should shut up.

Me and Michael and Ryan promised we wouldn't tell anyone about Miss Lazar's weird toilet bowl plunger museum. If she found out that we knew, she would know we snuck into her secret room.

I looked over at the next table where Andrea and her annoying friends sit. It had been a really long time since I bothered her, so I thought that maybe I should bother her to stay in practice.

The only problem was, Andrea had this sad look on her face. She looked so worried, I didn't want to shoot a straw wrapper at her or even hit her on the head with an empty milk carton. Andrea saw me looking, and she came over to our table with her annoying friend Emily.

"I'm worried about Mr. Klutz," she said.

"What about him?" I asked.

"I think he's depressed," Andrea said. "I think he's jealous of Miss Lazar."

"What?" Ryan said. "You're crazy."

"Did you see the look on his face when Miss Lazar unclogged the toilet?" Andrea asked. "And when she climbed up to the roof? Did you ever see how he looks when we all cheer for Miss Lazar?"

"He does look kind of sad," I agreed.

"My mother is a psychologist," Andrea

said. "She told me all about this stuff. I think Mr. Klutz is depressed because the principal is supposed to rule the school, but everybody acts like Miss Lazar is the big hero all the time. It's almost like Miss Lazar is the *real* principal."

"You're right," said Michael.

"We've got to do something," said Emily.

We thought and thought and thought about what we could do to cheer up Mr. Klutz. Andrea said we should do something that would make Mr. Klutz feel like a hero for a change. Ryan said we should start an emergency. Michael remembered that Miss Lazar has the day off every

Wednesday, and today was Wednesday. If we started an emergency, Mr. Klutz would have to be the hero.

If there's one thing I'm good at, it's starting emergencies. So I tried to think of an emergency I could start. That's when I got the greatest idea in the history of the world.

"Mr. Klutz said he used to be a rock climber, right?" I asked. "And when Miss Lazar climbed up the school, he said it was simple rock climbing. Well, let's throw something up on the roof of the school. Then we can ask Mr. Klutz to get it!"

"That's a dumb idea," said Michael.

"That's the dumbest idea in the history of the world," said Ryan.

"A.J., you're a genius!" said Andrea.

"Oooooh!" Ryan said. "A.J. and Andrea are in *love!*"

"When are you gonna get married?" asked Michael.

"Shut up," I said.

A New Hero

Luckily it was a nice day, so we had outside recess. We all went out to the playground. Andrea said we could throw her lunch box up on the roof of the school.

I'm the best thrower, so I got the job of throwing Andrea's lunch box up on the roof. The first couple of tries, I didn't reach the roof, and the lunch box almost hit a window on the second floor. It's hard to throw a lunch box! But finally, on the third try, I got the lunch box up on the roof.

Next we had to get Mr. Klutz. We rushed into school and went down the hall to his office. Mr. Klutz's office is really cool. He has a big snowboarding poster on the wall and a Foosball table in the corner. When we came in, he was wearing his boxing shorts and punching his punching bag. Mr. Klutz is really good at sports.

We decided that Andrea should do the talking, because she takes acting lessons after school. And it was *her* lunch box that was up on the roof.

"Mr. Klutz!" she said. "We have an emergency! A.J. threw my lunch box up on the roof! My lunch was in it! If I don't eat my lunch, I'll starve and die! We need your help!"

Andrea is a really good actress. She should be in movies.

"I'm so hungry," added Andrea, rubbing her tummy.

"Why did you throw Andrea's lunch box up on the roof, A.J.?" asked Mr. Klutz.

I didn't think Mr. Klutz was going to ask that. He looked at me. I looked at Andrea. Why did she have to go and tell Mr. Klutz I was the one who threw her lunch box up on the roof? Andrea looked at me too. I didn't know what to say. I didn't know what to do. I had to think fast.

"My invisible friend told me to do it," I said.

"Your invisible friend?" said Mr. Klutz.

"Hey, you never told us you had an invisible friend, A.J.," said Michael.

"Yeah, what's your invisible friend's name?" asked Ryan.

Actually, I wasn't *completely* lying. I *used* to have an invisible friend. But me and my invisible friend got into an argument one day, and after that we weren't friends anymore. I just used him to blame stuff on when I made mistakes.

"It doesn't matter what the invisible friend's name is!" said Andrea. "Mr. Klutz, we need you to climb up on the roof and get my lunch box. Please, please, pleeeeeese?"

At first Mr. Klutz didn't want to do it. But I guess Andrea was such a good actress that he took off his boxing gloves and followed us out to the playground. He looked up at the wall of the school.

"It doesn't look too difficult," Mr. Klutz said. "I used to climb walls like this all the time in my younger days."

"I bet you can do it," I said.

Mr. Klutz dug his toe into a crack

between two bricks and started pulling himself up the wall.

"Look!" one of the kids in the playground shouted. "Mr. Klutz is climbing the school!"

All the kids at recess came over to watch. Mr. Klutz was a fast climber. He was already halfway up to the roof.

"It's working like a charm!" Andrea whispered. "Mr. Klutz will be the hero!"

Mr. Klutz got all the way up to the top and climbed on the roof. He found

Andrea's lunch box and tossed it down.

"Hooray!" we all started shouting. "Hooray for Mr. Klutz! Hip hip hooray! He's our hero!"

Mr. Klutz turned around and started lowering himself from the roof. He got a few feet down, and then suddenly he stopped.

"What's the matter, Mr. Klutz?" somebody shouted.

"I—I'm stuck!" he yelled.

11

Another Emergency

Mr. Klutz was just hanging there off the side of the school, a few feet from the top. We all gasped. Somebody ran to get Miss Daisy and Mrs. Cooney, the school nurse. Miss Daisy had helped us once before, when Mr. Klutz got stuck on the top of the flagpole and had to be lowered down.

"You're doing great!" Andrea shouted up to Mr. Klutz. "Keep going!"

"I can't!" Mr. Klutz yelled down.

"Then go up to the top!" Ryan shouted up.

"I can't!" Mr. Klutz yelled down.

"Why not?" we all shouted up.

"I'm afraid I'll fall!" Mr. Klutz yelled down.

I guess it's a lot easier to climb *up* a wall than it is to climb back *down* a wall. Mr. Klutz was frozen up there. He couldn't move.

By that time the whole school was outside watching him. Miss Small, our gym teacher, had some kids go get a bunch of tumbling mats from the gym. She put them on the ground below Mr. Klutz so if he fell, he wouldn't end up like Humpty Dumpty.

"This is all your fault, A.J.!" said Andrea. "You're the one who said we should start an emergency."

"Hey, you're the one who said he was depressed!" I told Andrea. "And you said I was a genius. It's your fault."

"Is not!"

"Is too!"

We went on like that for a while, until Mrs. Cooney said she was going to call the fire department on her cell phone. They could bring over a long ladder and rescue Mr. Klutz.

Call Miss Lazar!

"Don't call the fire department!" yelled down Mr. Klutz.

"Why not?" asked Mrs. Cooney.

"I play racquetball with the fire chief once a week," Mr. Klutz yelled down. "If he finds out about this, he'll never let me hear the end of it."

"So what should we do?" asked Miss Daisy.

"Call Miss Lazar!" yelled down Mr. Klutz.

"But it's her day off," said Miss Daisy.

"Just call her!"

Hooray for Miss Lazar!

It was the most amazing sight in the history of the world! Mr. Klutz was hanging off the side of the school. He could fall at any moment. And we would get to see it, live and in person. It was a real Kodak moment. You should have been there!

One of the teachers ran to the office to

get Miss Lazar's home phone number. Mrs. Cooney called the number on her cell phone.

"Tell her to hurry!" yelled down Mr. Klutz. "I can't hang on here forever!"

It was about a million hundred hours until we heard the sound of Miss Lazar's scooter buzzing up the street. She screeched to a halt and hopped off. Everybody cheered.

"This looks like a job for Super Custodian!" said Miss Lazar. "How did you get up there, Mr. Klutz?"

"Never mind that," he yelled. "How am I going to get *down*?"

Miss Lazar looked at the wall. She

looked at Mr. Klutz. Then she looked at me.

"A.J.," she said, "remember the secret room I showed you in my office? I need you to run down there as fast as you can. Open the door and get my blue plunger. It has a hole in the wooden handle."

"Why do you want a toilet plunger *now*?" I asked.

"Go!" Miss Lazar said. "Duty calls!"

Miss Lazar said "duty" again.

I ran as fast as I could to Miss Lazar's office. I grabbed the blue plunger from the wall in the secret room. When I ran back out to the playground with it, Miss Lazar had already climbed up to the roof of the school. She had a rope in her hand. Mr. Klutz was still hanging off the wall, a few feet below her.

"Throw me the plunger, A.J.!" Miss Lazar yelled.

I threw the plunger up on the roof, being careful not to hit Mr. Klutz with it. Miss Lazar tied the rope to the plunger.

"What's she doing?" somebody asked.

"Who knows?" Michael said.

Miss Lazar leaned over the edge of the

roof with the toilet bowl plunger in her hand.

"Okay, Mr. Klutz," she said. "I need you to hold steady. I'm going to mash this plunger against the top of your head."

"What?!" yelled Mr. Klutz.

"After the plunger is stuck to your head," said Miss Lazar, "I'll be able to lower you down to the ground."

"That's crazy," said Miss Daisy, "but it just might work!"

Miss Lazar jammed the plunger against Mr. Klutz's shiny bald head until it stuck there.

"Does it feel like it's on good and tight?" asked Miss Lazar.

"Yes!" said Mr. Klutz. "But this is very embarrassing."

"Don't worry about that," said Miss Lazar. "Now I want you to let go of the wall with your hands and feet."

"I'm scared!" said Mr. Klutz.

"I've got you!" shouted Miss Lazar.

Mr. Klutz let go of the wall. Miss Lazar held the rope tight. The plunger stuck to Mr. Klutz's head like glue. Slowly Miss Lazar began lowering Mr. Klutz down with the rope.

"It's working!" somebody shouted.

I'll say this much—you never know when one of those toilet bowl plunger thingies might come in handy.

"Mr. Klutz sure is lucky that he's bald!" said Andrea.

"Wow!" said Ryan. "That plunger really sucks!"

Little by little, Miss Lazar let out the rope until Mr. Klutz's feet touched the ground. Then Miss Lazar climbed down the wall herself, and everybody started cheering and clapping.

"Hooray for Miss Lazar!" kids were shouting. "Hip hip hooray! She's a real superhero!"

"Thanks, Miss Lazar," said Mr. Klutz. "You saved my life!"

"It's all in a day's work," said Miss Lazar as she got back on her scooter. "Even on my day off! But now I must take my leave. You kids better get back to class. Duty calls!"

Miss Lazar had said "duty" again.

After she buzzed away on her scooter, Mr. Klutz pulled at the plunger, but it was stuck to his head pretty tightly. He said he didn't mind, because it had saved his life. But he would look really funny in hats for a while.

All the excitement was

over, and we had to go back inside boring old Ella Mentry School.

Maybe someday we'll find out if Miss Lazar is a real superhero or not. Maybe someday Mr. Klutz will get over his jealousy of Miss Lazar. Maybe someday we'll find out who put the crayons down the toilet. Maybe someday we'll find out what chicken pox has to do with chickens. Maybe someday Mr. Klutz will get the toilet bowl plunger off his head. Maybe someday I'll be able to hear the word "duty" and not start giggling.

But it won't be easy!